Dear Parent:

Congratulations! Your child is taking the first steps on an exciting journey. The destination? Independent reading!

STEP INTO READING® will help your child get there. The program offers books at five levels that accompany children from their first attempts at reading to reading success. Each step includes fun stories, fiction and nonfiction, and colorful art. There are also Step into Reading Sticker Books, Step into Reading Math Readers, and Step into Reading Phonics Readers— a complete literacy program with something to interest every child.

Learning to Read, Step by Step!

Ready to Read Preschool–Kindergarten
• big type and easy words • rhyme and rhythm • picture clues
For children who know the alphabet and are eager to begin reading.

Reading with Help Preschool–Grade 1
• basic vocabulary • short sentences • simple stories
For children who recognize familiar words and sound out new words with help.

Reading on Your Own Grades 1–3
• engaging characters • easy-to-follow plots • popular topics
For children who are ready to read on their own.

Reading Paragraphs Grades 2–3
• challenging vocabulary • short paragraphs • exciting stories
For newly independent readers who read simple sentences with confidence.

Ready for Chapters Grades 2–4
• chapters • longer paragraphs • full-color art
For children who want to take the plunge into chapter books but still like colorful pictures.

STEP INTO READING® is designed to give every child a successful reading experience. The grade levels are only guides. Children can progress through the steps at their own speed, developing confidence in their reading, no matter what their grade.

Remember, a lifetime love of reading starts with a single step!

Copyright © 1998, 2003 Disney Enterprises, Inc. Based on the "Winnie the Pooh" works by A. A. Milne and E. H. Shepard. All rights reserved. Published in the United States by Random House Children's Books, a division of Random House, Inc., New York, and simultaneously in Canada by Random House of Canada Limited, Toronto, in conjunction with Disney Enterprises, Inc. Originally published in different form by Disney Press in 1998. First Random House Edition 2003.

www.stepintoreading.com

Educators and librarians, for a variety of teaching tools, visit us at
www.randomhouse.com/teachers

Library of Congress Cataloging-in-Publication Data
Gaines, Isabel.
Pooh's Halloween pumpkin / by Isabel Gaines; illustrated by
Josie Yee.—1st Random House ed.
        p. cm.—(Step into reading. A Step 2 book)
Rev. ed. of: Pooh's pumpkin. 1998.
SUMMARY: As Pooh eats honey and watches the seed he has planted, he wonders if it will ever become a pumpkin.
ISBN 0-7364-2160-2 (trade)—ISBN 0-7364-8023-4 (lib. bdg.)
[1. Pumpkins—Fiction. 2. Teddy bears—Fiction. 3. Toys—Fiction.]
I. Yee, Josie, ill. II. Gaines, Isabel. Pooh's pumpkin.
III. Title. IV. Series: Step into reading. Step 2 Book.
PZ7.G1277Pofv 2003 [E]—dc21 2002012826

Printed in the United States of America   10 9 8 7 6 5 4 3 2 1

STEP INTO READING, RANDOM HOUSE, and the Random House colophon are registered trademarks of Random House, Inc.

STEP INTO READING®

STEP 2

Disney

Winnie the Pooh

Pooh's Halloween Pumpkin

By Isabel Gaines

Illustrated by Josie Yee

Random House 🏠 New York

One spring day,
Christopher Robin
and Pooh saw
Rabbit planting seeds.

"What are
you planting?"
asked Pooh.
"Pumpkin seeds,"
said Rabbit.

"I want to
grow a pumpkin,
too," said Pooh.
"Growing a pumpkin
is hard work,"
said Rabbit.

"I will take
good care of it,"
promised Pooh.
So Rabbit gave
him a seed.

Christopher Robin
and Pooh
planted the seed
in a sunny spot.

"I will watch
the pumpkin
grow," said Pooh.

"But the pumpkin
will not be ready
until the fall,"
said Christopher Robin.
"I will wait,"
said Pooh.

"First I need
something to eat,"
said Pooh.
So Pooh went home.
He took all his
honey outside.

Pooh watched the spot
where the seed
was planted.
Pooh ate and watched
and ate some more.

Soon it was summer.

Piglet came along.

"What a pretty vine

you are growing, Pooh!"

said Piglet.

"But I wanted
a pumpkin,
not a vine,"
said Pooh.

Pooh watched the vine.

He ate some honey.

Pooh ate and watched

and ate some more.

Soon the vine grew

a flower.

"I wanted a pumpkin,
not a flower!"
Pooh told Owl.
"Maybe you are not
growing a pumpkin,"
said Owl.

"You have a vine.

You have a flower.

I think you are

growing . . ."

"... a cucumber!"

said Owl.

"Do cucumbers
taste good
with honey?"
asked Pooh.

Pooh scratched
his head.
"A pumpkin seed
should grow into
a pumpkin," he said.

So Pooh watched
the plant.

He watered it.

He ate more honey.

One day, Pooh woke
from a nap.
The air was cooler.
The leaves were
changing colors.

"There is a green
ball on your vine,"
said Eeyore.
"But I wanted a
pumpkin!" said Pooh.

"Oh, well,"
said Eeyore.
"I never get
what I want, either."

Weeks passed.

The green ball

grew bigger.

And so did

Pooh's tummy!

One day, part of
the ball turned
orange.

Soon all of the
ball was orange.
Leaves fell from
the trees.
There was a big
orange pumpkin
on Pooh's vine!

Everyone gathered
around Pooh's
pumpkin.

"The pumpkin looks
like your tummy!"
said Tigger.
"You grew with
the pumpkin!"
said Christopher Robin.

The friends decided
to carve the pumpkin
for Halloween.

"I will carve the eyes,"
said Owl.

"I will carve the nose,"
said Rabbit.

"And I will carve
the mouth,"
said Piglet.

Pooh's Halloween
pumpkin made
the best
jack-o'-lantern in
the Hundred-Acre Wood.